HOPSCOTCH TWISTY TALES

The Emperor's New Kit

by Maureen Haselhurst and Kelly Kennedy

W

FRANKLIN WATTS

LONDON•SYDNEY

This story is based on the traditional fairy tale,
The Emperor's New Clothes, but with a new twist.
You can read the original story in
Hopscotch Fairy Tales. Can you make
up your own twist for the story?

First published in 2013 by
Franklin Watts
338 Euston Road
London
NW1 3BH

Franklin Watts Australia
Level 17/207 Kent Street
Sydney
NSW 2000

A CIP catalogue record for this book is available
from the British Library.

ISBN 978 1 4451 1629 7 (hbk)
ISBN 978 1 4451 1635 8 (pbk)

Series Editor: Melanie Palmer
Series Advisor: Catherine Glavina
Series Designer: Peter Scoulding

Printed in China

Franklin Watts is a division of
Hachette Children's Books,
an Hachette UK company
www.hachette.co.uk

Enrico Empery was an ace footballer.
He was captain of Bootsville United.
He was so good that his fans
nicknamed him "The Emperor".

Enrico loved football, but he loved clothes almost as much. He wore expensive designer suits, shoes and shirts. Being rich and famous had made him a bit of a show-off.

5

Everyone admired "the Emperor" except for Frankie Foulo. Frankie was another star player at Bootsville United, but he knew he would never be as good as Enrico.

He watched Enrico being interviewed on television. "What a big-head," he muttered jealously. "Someone should teach him a lesson."

Bootsville United had reached the final of the cup.

"I need a new kit – something really special," said Enrico.

Designers from all over the world brought all kinds of trendy kits, but none of them was special enough for the Emperor.

As he watched, Frankie thought of a trick. "I'll make Enrico look really silly," he thought, smiling.

It was the day of the big match.
Frankie took his present to Enrico.

13

"I've found you an amazing kit," Frankie said craftily.
"It's very cool because only top footballers can see it. It's invisible to all the other players."

15

Enrico ripped open the box and looked inside. He couldn't see anything! He must be a bad player. He stared sadly at the invisible kit.

He would just have to pretend that he could see it. "It's great," he fibbed. "It's brilliant!" agreed the rest of the team, who couldn't see it either.

Sass, the team mascot, arrived and heard all about the amazing kit. But the cruel trick didn't fool her. She had to put a stop to it.

"I bet Frankie wishes he had a kit like that," she said to Enrico. "Why don't you swap with him?"

"No way!" yelled Frankie.

But the team thought it was a great idea. So it was Frankie Foulo who went onto the pitch dressed in the Emperor's invisible new kit.

All the crowd cheered as Frankie and the Emperor kicked the ball up into the air. The game was on.

Puzzle 1

Put these pictures in the correct order.
Which event do you think is most important?
Now try writing the story in your own words!

Puzzle 2

1. I hate show-offs.

2. I am good at spotting trouble.

3. I'm the best player!

4. I like making things fair.

5. I get jealous very easily.

6. I have lots of expensive clothes.

Choose the correct speech bubbles for each character. Can you think of any others? Turn over to find the answers.

Answers

Puzzle 1

The correct order is: 1c, 2e, 3f, 4b, 5a, 6d

Puzzle 2

The Emperor: 3, 6

Frankie Foulo: 1, 5

Sass: 2, 4

Look out for more Hopscotch Twisty Tales and Fairy Tales:

TWISTY TALES
The Lovely Duckling
ISBN 978 1 4451 1627 3*
ISBN 978 1 4451 1633 4
**Hansel and Gretel
and the Green Witch**
ISBN 978 1 4451 1628 0*
ISBN 978 1 4451 1634 1
The Emperor's New Kit
ISBN 978 1 4451 1629 7*
ISBN 978 1 4451 1635 8
**Rapunzel and the
Prince of Pop**
ISBN 978 1 4451 1630 3*
ISBN 978 1 4451 1636 5
**Dick Whittington
Gets on his Bike**
ISBN 978 1 4451 1631 0*
ISBN 978 1 4451 1637 2
**The Pied Piper and
the Wrong Song**
ISBN 978 1 4451 1632 7*
ISBN 978 1 4451 1638 9
**The Princess and the
Frozen Peas**
ISBN 978 1 4451 0675 5
Snow White Sees the Light
ISBN 978 1 4451 0676 2

**The Elves and the Trendy
Shoes**
ISBN 978 1 4451 0678 6
The Three Frilly Goats Fluff
ISBN 978 1 4451 0677 9
Princess Frog
ISBN 978 1 4451 0679 3
Rumpled Stilton Skin
ISBN 978 1 4451 0680 9
Jack and the Bean Pie
ISBN 978 1 4451 0182 8
**Brownilocks and the Three
Bowls of Cornflakes**
ISBN 978 1 4451 0183 5
Cinderella's Big Foot
ISBN 978 1 4451 0184 2
Little Bad Riding Hood
ISBN 978 1 4451 0185 9
**Sleeping Beauty –
100 Years Later**
ISBN 978 1 4451 0186 6

FAIRY TALES
The Three Little Pigs
ISBN 978 0 7496 7905 7
Little Red Riding Hood
ISBN 978 0 7496 7907 1
Goldilocks and the Three Bears
ISBN 978 0 7496 7903 3
Hansel and Gretel
ISBN 978 0 7496 7904 0

Rapunzel
ISBN 978 0 7496 7906 4
Rumpelstiltskin
ISBN 978 0 7496 7908 8
The Elves and the Shoemaker
ISBN 978 0 7496 8543 0
The Ugly Duckling
ISBN 978 0 7496 8544 7
Sleeping Beauty
ISBN 978 0 7496 8545 4
The Frog Prince
ISBN 978 0 7496 8546 1
**The Princess and
the Pea**
ISBN 978 0 7496 8547 8
Dick Whittington
ISBN 978 0 7496 8548 5
Cinderella
ISBN 978 0 7496 7417 5
Snow White
ISBN 978 0 7496 7418 2
**The Pied Piper
of Hamelin**
ISBN 978 0 7496 7419 9
Jack and the Beanstalk
ISBN 978 0 7496 7422 9
The Three Billy Goats Gruff
ISBN 978 0 7496 7420 5
The Emperor's New Clothes
ISBN 978 0 7496 7421 2